Nathan the Nipper

Michael Wagner

Contents

Nathan the Nipper
Hi there! I'm Nathan and I'm a "nipper".
LIFEGUARD

Being a nipper means
I'm a **junior** surf lifesaver.

Every summer, nippers spend a lot of time at beaches. Beaches can be dangerous.

Nipper Facts

- There are about 50 000 nippers in Australia.
- Nippers are between 5 and 13 years old.
- Younger nippers learn about beach safety and play games.
- Older nippers play beach sports.

Beach Safety

Lifesavers save thousands of people every year in Australia.

As a nipper, I have learned a lot about beach safety with **FLAGS**!

Find the red and yellow flags and swim between them.

Look at the safety signs at the beach.

Ask a lifesaver if it's safe to swim.

Get someone else to swim with you.

Stick your hand up if you're in trouble.

The Red and Yellow Flags

Red and yellow flags show the safest part of the beach to swim in. Swim between the flags!

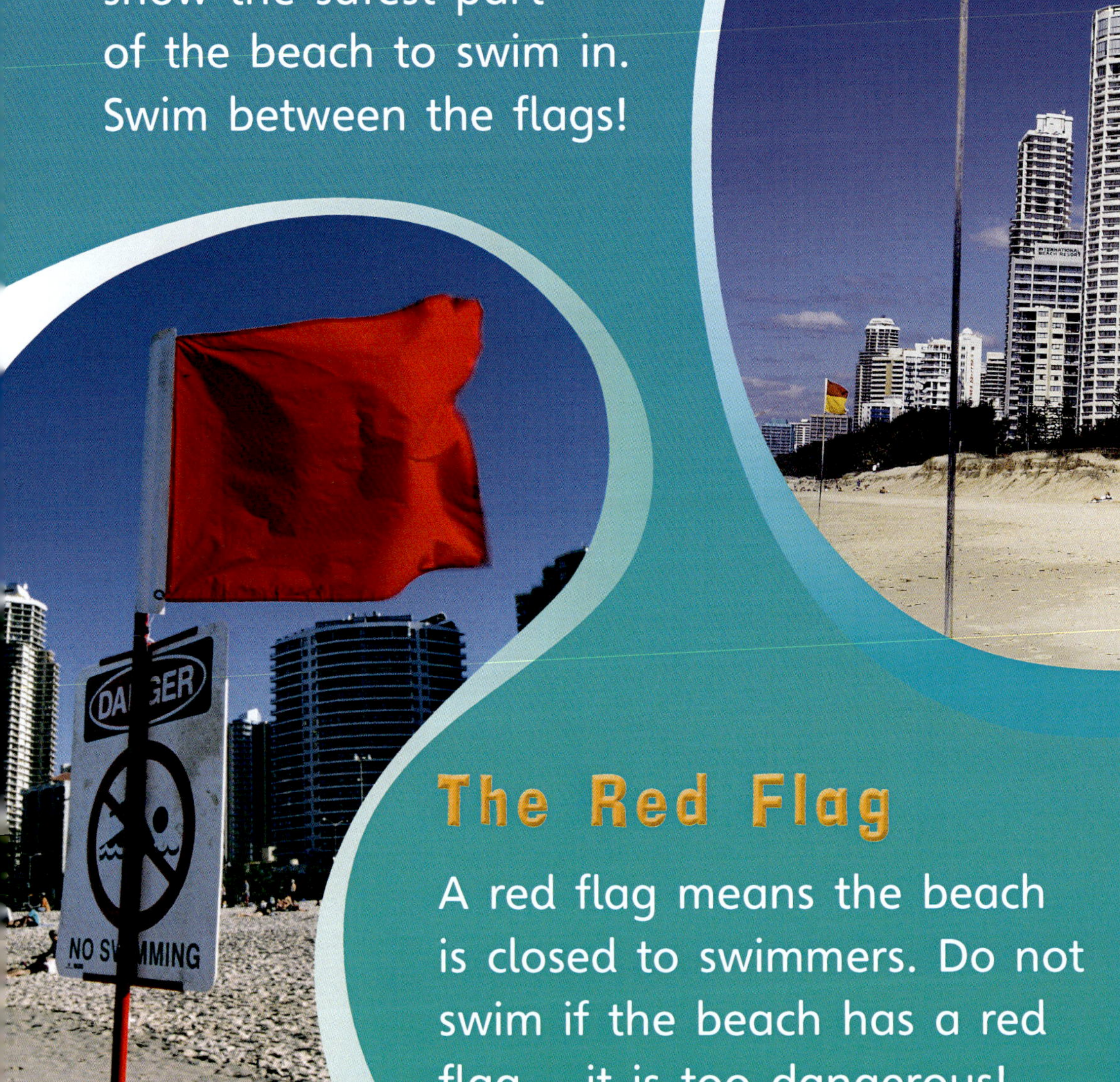

The Red Flag

A red flag means the beach is closed to swimmers. Do not swim if the beach has a red flag – it is too dangerous!

Never!

- Never swim at a beach that has no lifesavers.
- Never swim at night.
- Never run and dive into the water.
- Never swim straight after eating.

Beach Danger

A rip is a strong flow of water that is going back out to sea. It can look like a very **calm** part of the sea.

A rip is often found between lots of crashing waves.

Rip Spotting

Can you see the rip between the waves?

Learning how to spot a rip will keep you much safer at the beach.

Don't Get Ripped!

A rip can take you out to sea – even if you are a good swimmer. If you are caught in a rip, you may find yourself far from the beach. It will be too hard to swim back to shore.

KEEPING SAFE IN A RIP

1 Stay calm.
2 Do not try to swim back to shore. You'll just get tired.
3 Wave your arms to tell everyone you need help.
4 Float on your back until someone comes to save you.

You Can Swim Out of a Rip

If you are in a rip, don't try to swim back to shore. If you swim sideways to the beach, you might be able to swim out of the rip. Then, the waves can help take you back in to shore.

The Day I Became a Nipper

One morning, there was a rip at our beach. I saw a boy get taken out by it.

I was with Mum when the boy started waving his arms. He was a long way from shore and was getting taken out to sea.

I was about to tell Mum when a surf lifesaver ran past me.

The lifesaver swam to the boy and put a rescue tube around him. He kept the boy's head out of the water.

Then, the lifesaver **towed** the boy out of the rip and back to the beach.

At the beach, the lifesaver lay the boy down. He checked to see if he was okay.

After a little while, the boy
sat up. He was okay but very tired.

The boy's parents thanked the lifesaver for saving their son. They even gave him a big hug!

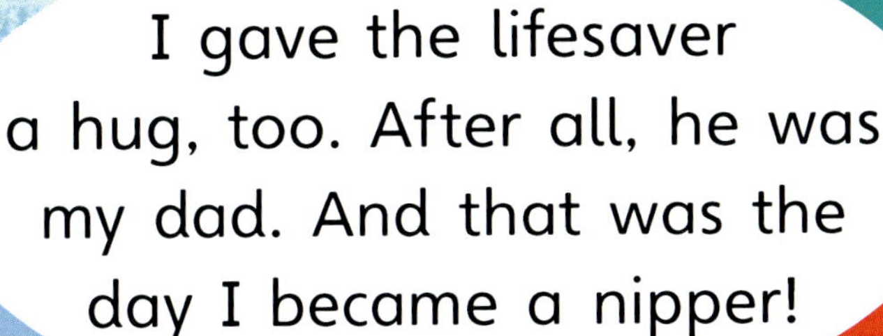

How to Become a Nipper

If you want to become a nipper like me, just go to your nearest surf lifesaving club.

Go on a Sunday morning in summer and ask to join up!

Glossary

calm not rough

junior younger

rip a strong flow of water moving out to sea

towed pulled using a rope

Index